Sto

HORATIO'S BIRTHDAY

Eleanor Clymer

HORATIO'S BIRTHDAY

ILLUSTRATED BY

Robert Quackenbush

ATHENEUM *1976* NEW YORK

Library of Congress Cataloging in Publication Data

Clymer, Eleanor Lowenton. Horatio's birthday.

SUMMARY: *Finding the house too quiet after Mrs. Casey's other pets grow up and leave home, Horatio begins to mope until he finds a way to remedy the situation.*
[1. Cats—Fiction] l. Quackenbush, Robert. ll. Title.
PZ7.C6272Hm [E] 76–89
ISBN *0–689–30520–6*

For Becky/E.C.

*For the 200 Block
East 78th Street, NYC and
To My Son*/R.Q.

HORATIO was a large, middle-aged, striped cat. He lived with a lady named Mrs. Casey in a brick house on a city street. Mrs. Casey took good care of him. She fed him the best liver in his own special bowl, and tuna fish on Sundays. She was very kind. In fact, Horatio sometimes thought she was too kind. She had been known to take in stray animals who had no place to live. There had been a pigeon with a broken wing. There was a rabbit, a puppy named Sam, and two lively kittens. They had annoyed Horatio by jumping on him and trying to make him play with them. Horatio often wished for peace and quiet.

Now, all of a sudden, it was very quiet in the house. The pigeon had flown away and made a nest on a nearby roof.

The rabbit had gone to live with Michael and Betsy, the children next door.

Sam the puppy was a grown-up dog and slept a lot. And the kittens were grown-up cats and lived with three little girls in the next block.

When her work was done, Mrs. Casey sat by the fire with her knitting. She was making little sweaters for her twin grandchildren. Sam snoozed at her feet. Horatio had nothing to do. He scratched at the door, and Mrs. Casey let him out. In a few minutes he said, "Meow!" and she let him in again.

"What's the matter, Horatio?" she asked. "It's nice and quiet here. Isn't that what you like?"

That was the trouble. It was *too* quiet.

"I don't know what to do about Horatio," said Mrs. Casey to Michael and Betsy one day. "I think he's bored."

"Poor Horatio," said Betsy. "How can we cheer him up?"

"I don't know," said Mrs. Casey. "His birthday is next week. I thought I'd make him a tuna fish pie. That's his favorite food, you know."

"Let's have a party for him," said Michael.

"Oh, good," said Mrs. Casey. "I'll ask my daughter and the twins. That should liven things up."

So the next week, Mrs. Casey's daughter came with her children. She had to bring quite a few things with her in the car. She brought toys, blankets, and clothes. She brought a playpen, two folding cribs, and a large box of baby food. The house was stuffed with things.

Mrs. Casey was proud of the twins. "Look, Horatio, aren't they sweet?" she asked.

They weren't bad, for babies. They didn't pull his whiskers. They just patted him gently and said, "Kitty!"

But they crawled about the living room and threw their toys all around, and all the neighbors came to admire them.

Mrs. Casey spent a lot of time in the kitchen cooking extra food. She also made a tuna fish pie, but wouldn't let Horatio have any.

And when night came, she moved out of her bedroom so the twins could have it. Their mother slept in the small bedroom. Mrs. Casey slept on the sofa. There was no place for Horatio at her feet. He had to sleep in the kitchen.

Horatio didn't like it a bit. He didn't know it was his birthday. But he felt this was not the way to treat him.

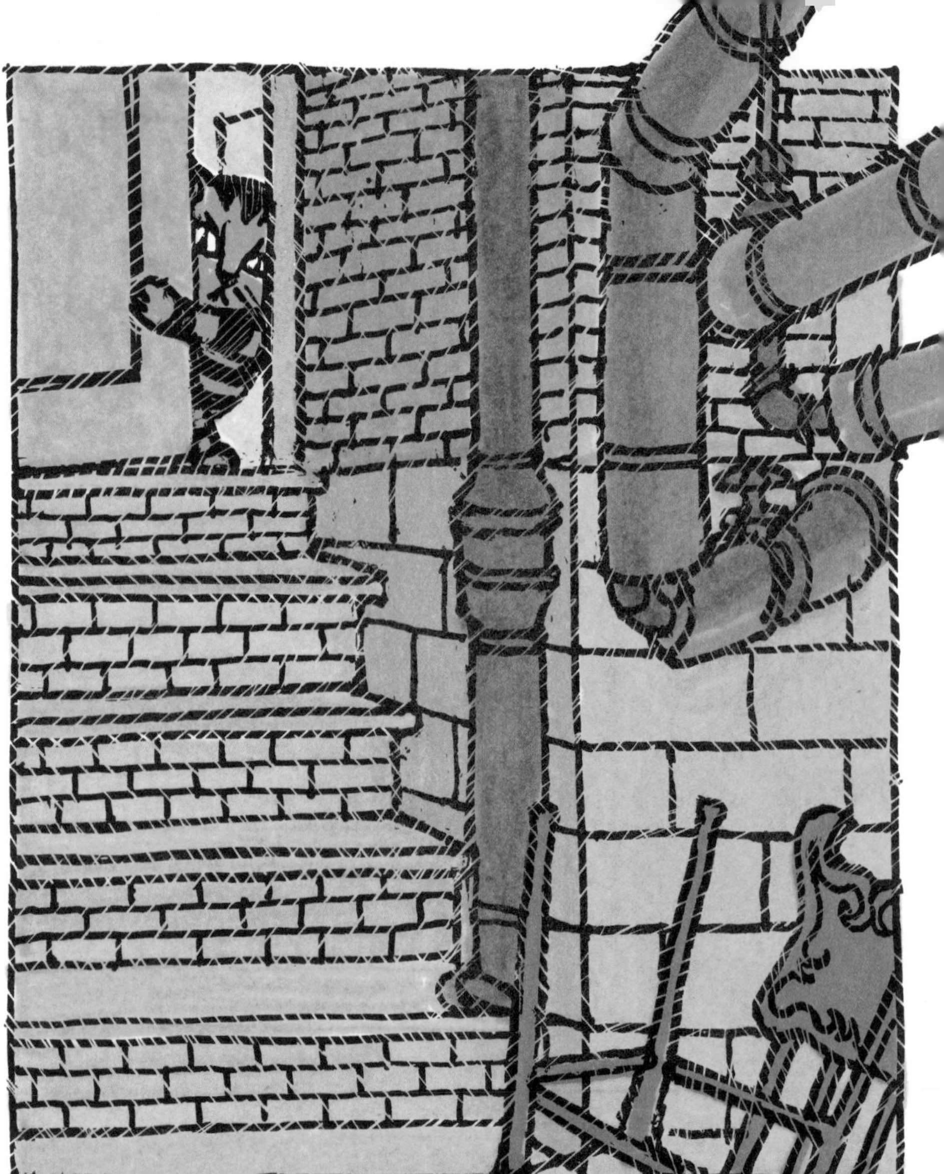

He curled up on his cushion by the stove and tried to sleep. But he couldn't. He got up and prowled around. He reached under the refrigerator with his paw and found a little ball that the kittens had left behind. He batted it about for a while. But it was boring, having nobody to admire him.

Then he noticed something. The door to the cellar was not closed. He put his paw around the edge and pulled it open. He ran downstairs. The door swung shut behind him.

Horatio wasn't allowed in the cellar. There were shelves full of jars and flowerpots, and Mrs. Casey was afraid he might knock something over. How silly; Horatio *never* knocked anything over. Only dogs did that.

He sniffed in all the corners. He peered behind some boxes. He walked carefully along the edges of the shelves.

Suddenly the furnace went on. It roared like a big, fat monster. Horatio backed away from it.

Then he saw something moving. A little gray face with black eyes and whiskers peered out from under the lowest shelf. It saw Horatio and disappeared. Horatio waited. He didn't really want to catch a mouse, though it would be fun to chase one.

But the mouse was gone.

Horatio poked his head under the shelf. In the wall he saw a hole. It was a big hole, big enough for a cat to get through. Perhaps a pipe had once gone through it.

Horatio squeezed into the hole. It was a tight fit, but he pushed himself through and found himself in the back yard!

The moon was shining. It was a fine night to be out. Horatio walked around the yard, scratched on a tree, and ate a sprig of catnip, which Mrs. Casey had planted for him.

There was a shed in the yard, and suddenly he saw that on top of it a little yellow cat was sitting. She looked silvery in the moonlight. On the ground were three other cats: a black cat, a gray and white cat, and a Siamese.

"Hello," Horatio said.

The cats looked at him. "Hello, Grandpa," said the black one.

"What are you doing here?" Horatio asked.

"We're just leaving," said the black cat. "We only stopped here to see if there was anything to eat, but there isn't."

"Of course there isn't," Horatio said to himself. "Mrs. Casey never leaves food around."

"Where are you going?" he asked.

"Oh, all over the neighborhood," said the black cat.

"Maybe I'll go with you," said Horatio.

"All right, Grandpa," said the black cat, "if you can keep up with us."

"Of course I can," said Horatio, "and don't call me Grandpa."

They started out. They leaped on top of the shed and down into the next yard. Horatio leaped, too.

"I can still jump," he thought.

They sniffed at a trash can, but the lid was on tight. They leaped up on top of a fence and ran along it to the next yard. The yellow cat stayed close to Horatio, but the others were far ahead.

At last they found a trash can with the lid off. They jumped into it and clawed away some pieces of paper.

"Here's something good!" said the black cat, pulling out a chicken wing.

The others tried to grab it away from him, but he growled at them. Soon they were off again, running along the fences.

"This is fun," thought Horatio, panting for breath.

"Hurry up, Grandpa," the black cat called.

Horatio had never done anything like this before. He had always led a quiet life. These cats seemed very wild and brave. But he wished he could find something to eat, too. He was getting hungry. He hadn't eaten much supper.

The little yellow cat stayed close beside him. Horatio stopped for a minute to catch his breath. He looked down into the yard below him. There was a cardboard box with something in it. Horatio jumped down and poked at it. Out fell a big piece of leftover turkey.

"Have some," he said to the yellow cat.

They sat down and chewed at the turkey together. Suddenly a light went on, and a lady came out of the house with a broom.

"Scat!" she shouted.

Horatio ran. What manners! He wasn't used to being spoken to like that. The yellow cat ran with him till they caught up with the others.

"Were you scared, Grandpa?" asked the black cat.

"I'm not your Grandpa," said Horatio crossly. "And I wasn't scared."

"Why don't we sing," said the Siamese cat. "I have a lovely voice."

"Oh, is that so!" said the gray and white cat. "Let's hear you."

They all sat on a roof and howled. Horatio thought it sounded very fine.

But some of the people in the houses didn't think so. A man opened a window and threw a bucket of water at them.

"Yow!" they squalled, and they jumped down into the next yard. But here they had an even worse surprise. A huge black dog ran out of the house, barking horribly.

"Run!" yelled the black cat, and quick as a flash he climbed the fence and was gone. The gray and the Siamese ran, too. Only Horatio and the yellow cat were left.

"Wow! Wow!" barked the dog, showing his fierce teeth.

"Help!" cried the yellow cat.

"Run!" Horatio ordered. "I'll take care of him." And he waited till the dog was almost on him.

"Take that!" he growled, and flashing his claws he gave the dog a scratch on the nose.

"Ow! Ow!" howled the dog, and it turned and ran.

"Now follow me," said Horatio. He leaped up on a fence and ran along it till he came to Mrs. Casey's shed, then down into the yard and through his private hole.

"Where are we?" asked the yellow cat, trembling.

"This is where I live," said Horatio, curling up on a pile of newspapers.

She curled up beside him. "My, you were brave!" she said.

Horatio breathed hard for a while. Then they both went to sleep.

In the morning, Michael and Betsy came for the party. It was to be a breakfast party. The twins were awake and dressed. The table was set with Horatio's tuna pie in the place of honor; and the presents were all ready: a catnip mouse, a new cushion, a box of cat candy.

But where was Horatio?

He wasn't in his bed in the kitchen. He wasn't in the living room. Mrs. Casey opened the back door and called. He wasn't in the yard. Anyway, how could he have gotten out?

Suddenly Betsy said, "I thought I heard him."

They all kept quiet. "Meow!" came from behind the cellar door.

"The cellar!" said Mrs. Casey. "How did he get in there?" She pulled open the door. There was Horatio.

"Happy birthday!" they shouted. "Come and see your presents."

But Horatio acted as if he had not heard. He turned and ran back into the cellar. What was the matter with him?

In a minute he was back. And with him was a little yellow cat.

"Well, Horatio!" said Mrs. Casey. "Who is this? And how did she get into the cellar?"

Horatio didn't answer. That was *his* secret.

The little cat, seeing all those people, looked scared. She looked as if she wanted to run away. Mrs. Casey picked her up and patted her.

"You're very pretty," she said. "But where do you live? Haven't you got a home?"

Horatio was getting tired of all these questions. What about something to eat.

He went and sat in front of the refrigerator.

"Meow!" he said loudly.

"You're hungry!" said Mrs. Casey. And she divided the tuna pie in two and put it in two dishes. She poured milk into a pie pan. Horatio and the yellow cat ate and drank. Then they washed their faces.

The others sat down to breakfast. Afterward Horatio was allowed to see his presents. He tore the paper off the catnip mouse. He would have liked to put it away until later, but to please them he bit it and rolled over a few times. He nibbled a piece of cat candy and let the yellow cat have some.

But the present he liked best was the new cushion. He curled up on it, with the yellow cat beside him, and they both purred happily.

Mrs. Casey looked down at them and smiled.

"Horatio was lonesome," she said. "He brought someone home to play with. But where did she come from?"

"I think I know," said Betsy. "She lived with some people across the street. They moved away and left her."

"What a shame!" said Mrs. Casey. "Then she can stay here. I'll call her Goldilocks. But how did she get into the cellar?"

Horatio opened one eye and looked at her. Maybe someday he would show her, but not now.

"Meow!" he said and went to sleep.